tim the tiny horse at large

Harry Hill used to be a doctor but not for

a long time now. He's had many TV shows

and he tells jokes for a living. His hobbies

are painting and drawing and occasional games

of swingball.

Also by Harry Hill

Tim the Tiny Horse

Further Adventures of the Queen Mum

Harry Hill's Whopping Great Joke Book

tim the tiny horse at large

ff

FABER AND FABER

For Ava Rae Taylor – Tim's biggest fan

First published in 2008
by Faber and Faber Ltd
Bloomsbury House
74-77 Great Russell Street
London WCIB 3DA
This paperback edition first published in 2009

Printed in Italy by L.E.G.O S.p.A.
Design and colour work by Ken de Silva

A CIP record for this book
Is available from the British Library

ISBN 978-0-571-24415-7

2 4 6 8 10 9 7 5 3 1

Contents

the
adventure
continues

A lot has happened to
Tim the Tiny Horse since we
last caught up with him.
But if you were hoping that
maybe he'd got bigger...

then I'm afraid I must
disappoint you. Tim is <u>still</u>
a very small horse.

Tim the Tiny Horse

A tic tac

Diagram to show relative size
of Tim the Tiny Horse

So small is he in fact that he <u>could</u>
use an iPod as his main T.V., with
the headphones as speakers (his
ears are too small to need a
sub-woofer) ... but he doesn't.

9

He is so small that he could
use an acorn cup as a basin,
but chooses not to.

As he doesn't really go for
that Rustic Look.

He is so small that on
one occasion, whilst
eating some spaghetti hoops...

he got one caught over
his nose... and it acted...
as a __muzzle__!

He had to get
his best friend
(who is a fly)
to bite it off.

which was a little embarrassing
for both of them.

No, he still cuts a diminutive
figure around the town or
more commonly...

in his matchbox home.

Fly Gets
Married

One day Tim's best friend Fly
called to say that he had
important news.

'Fire away!' said Tim.

'No, this is not the sort of news
I can tell you over the phone...'
said Fly.

'I'll be over in five minutes.'

'Hmm,' thought Tim
the Tiny Horse...

'I wonder what Fly's news is?'

Perhaps he'd bought Tim
a present.

No, it wasn't Tim's birthday
for another month.

Bits of 'scratchy'

Perhaps Fly had come into some
money and wanted to share
his good fortune with Tim.

Tim immediately thought about what he would buy with his share...

and quickly settled on a fudge bar.

That would be **More** than enough.

He didn't want to be

GREEDY.

Fly didn't actually say
he had g<u>oo</u>d news though...

just :IMPORTANT: news.

maybe that's why
Fly hadn't felt able
to tell Tim the news...

over the phone.

Maybe Fly was
in some sort of
TROUBLE!

He was a bit of a
hot-head.

Maybe he was in a dispute
with a wasp over some
leftover food...

and was having to leave
town for a while to
allow things to cool off.

Just then, the doorbell rang.

It was Fly.

'I'm getting married!'
said Fly.

Tim pulled a face...*

He was really pleased
for Fly ...

*In fact, a series of faces.

but at the same time
was a little concerned.

After all Fly had only known
his girlfriend for a week.

This anxiety swirled around
in Tim's head...

as he thought about how
to react to the news.

Before he knew it, several seconds had passed.

'GREAT!'
said Tim the Tiny Horse
rather half-heartedly.

GREAT!

Unfortunately the pause...

and the face...

and the level of heartedness...

$$\text{(clock)} + \text{(horse face)} + \text{(heart)} = \text{?}$$

had said it all.

Tim the Tiny Horse Falls in Love

Tim the Tiny Horse <u>was</u> tiny.
To give you some idea he
was so small that every now
and then he'd stand on
an ice cube...

Grrrr!

and pretend to be
a polar bear.

Small of body, yes...

but oh so big-hearted!

A heart so big that it longed...

nay, yearned ...

to be loved.

Sadly the right lady horse
had never come along.

They were all ... well ...

a bit bossy ...

and frankly far too big...

During the planning of Fly's wedding Tim had to meet regularly with other members of Fly's family.

Including Fly's sister, Chenille.

Now although Tim had known
Chenille for some time he
had never really <u>noticed</u> her...

if you know
what I mean.

Now he found himself staring
at her, and what's more ...

she appeared to stare back.

This brought on feelings that Tim
didn't really understand —

Pumping chest out

Holding tummy in

his heart raced—indeed, galloped...

over hedges and fences.

His face went all red! *

* which on top of his natural blue
colour made purple which made
him look like he was choking
on something.

Tim the Tiny Horse couldn't sleep at night...

for thinking about Fly's sister.

'This must be LOVE,'
thought Tim the Tiny Horse.
And he immediately determined
to tell Chenille of his feelings
for her.

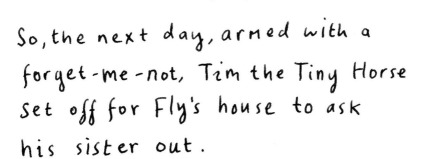

So, the next day, armed with a
forget-me-not, Tim the Tiny Horse
set off for Fly's house to ask
his sister out.

Unfortunately <u>Fly</u>. answered the door.

'Is your sister in?' asked Tim.

'Um... I think so...' said Fly,
a little confused.

Fly went and got his sister.

'This is for you,' said
Tim the Tiny Horse,
giving Chenille the
forget-me-not.

'I wondered
whether you'd like
   to go for a picnic
   sometime?'

'No ta!' said
Chenille, handing the
flower right back to Tim.

This Stumped Tim for
a moment.

'It was just... that I noticed
the way you looked at me,'
he continued.

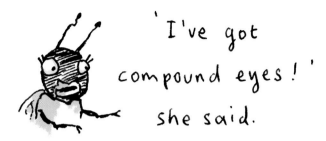

'I've got compound eyes!' she said.

'All us flies do, I look at everything all the time, don't read anything into that!'

It seemed he had totally misread the situation.

On the way home Tim felt
rather sad.

Then he thought about the
racing heart...

the purple face...

<u>and</u> that he'd never actually heard of a horse marrying a fly before.

'Oh well, better to have loved and lost!' thought Tim the Tiny Horse, and that night...

he slept like a log.

Tim's Best Friend's Wedding

After Tim had got over the initial shock of Fly's marriage plans—

(Fly had explained that because flies only tended to live about a year, in fact a week's courtship was perfectly respectable.

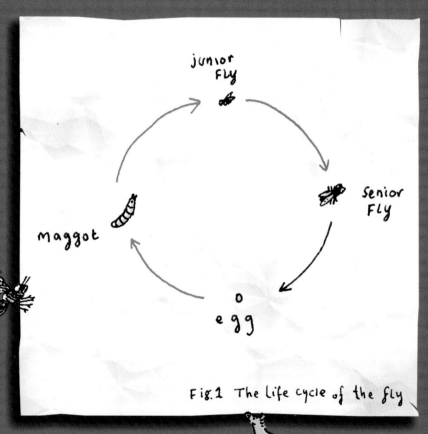

Fig.1 The life cycle of the fly

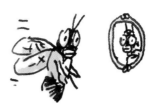

Plus he wasn't getting
any younger...

and you had to take
your opportunities where
you could.)

—Tim had some consolation from
Fly asking him to be ' Best Horse '.

Tim took this as the ultimate
endorsement of their friendship.

'What exactly does it entail?' said Tim the Tiny Horse.*

'There are various duties,' said Fly. 'But the main one is the Best Man's Speech!'

* He liked using the word tail in words.

Tim was so anxious at the thought
of this ...

that he staggered back...

tripped on a
hundred and thousand...

 ...and landed in
Fly's grandma's lap.

(Fly's grandma was now living
with Fly as she was unable to
cope on her own and was a risk
to herself from spiders)

chair lift

Big hairy
spider

'A speech! Quelle horreur!'
he thought, lapsing into French.

'Yes, it should be funny too.'
said Fly. 'But keep it clean.'

On the way home he bought a book called '101 Jokes For Your Best Man's Speech' by someone called Barry Cryer.

'Funny name for a comedian,' thought Tim the Tiny Horse.

As he read through it Tim realised that whilst being very funny some of the jokes were rather rude.

these two nuns go how's that! mother in stop get to bed she anything like 6. landed on his

HO HO HE HA
HAHAHAHA
HA HA HA HEEHE
HE HE E HEEHO HO

Tim the Tiny Horse laughed a lot...

but had a vision
of Fly's grandma

having a setback
if she ever heard them.

'You're on your own on this one,'
he thought to himself.

But he just couldn't think
of anything funny to say.

So he just wrote about why
he liked Fly and what
a good friend he was.

On the big day the speech went
down a storm.

Many of the guests had tears
in their eyes.

In fact it went down so well
that Tim decided to sling in one
of the jokes from the book...

(a particularly saucy one involving
an actress, a bishop... and a goat)

and Fly's grandma laughed so hard
she fell off her chair.

Mr & Mrs Fly Get a New Addition

Tim the Tiny Horse noticed that
Fly's new wife had put on a
little weight...

and that her breath had
started to smell of pickled
onions.

Well, you didn't have to be
Dr Robert Winston to work
out that this probably meant
that Fly's new wife was
going to have a MAGGOT.

'Indeed she is!'
beamed Fly, proudly.

'Congratulations!'
said Tim.

Although he <u>actually</u> thought
it was a little soon.

After all they'd only been
married a day and a half.

Tim hadn't even eaten his piece of wedding cake...

and the photos weren't even back from the printer's.

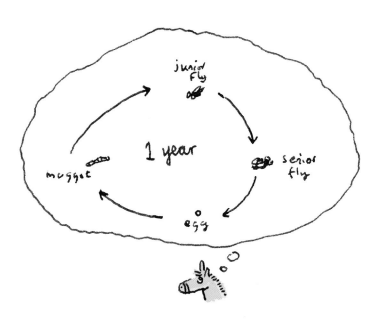

Then Tim remembered
the urgency of the fly's
life cycle...

and let it pass.

Fly and his wife set about
making their home more
baby friendly.

They installed a cot ...

bought a number
of soft toys...

and even painted the walls of
the nursery with well-known
fly children's characters
such as ...

Mickey Fly...

The
Telly-Flybbies...

and Flyddy
[the little fly...

with the red-and-yellow car].

In no time Fly's wife had given birth to a baby fly or 'Maggot'.

'He's got your nose!'
said Tim to Fly.

{closer}
{view}

{ Much
{ closer view}
{ so you can
{ see his face}

Everyone stared at Maggot, who rolled around on his blanket...

and who made noises...

from both ends.

Tim couldn't really see what this baby had to offer.

Then Maggot looked straight at Tim...

and <u>smiled</u>.

Tim smiled back.

Now he understood.

Tim the Tiny Horse Babysits for Fly

Tim the Tiny Horse felt rather
sorry for Fly and his wife...

the pair of them always
looked _so_ tired.

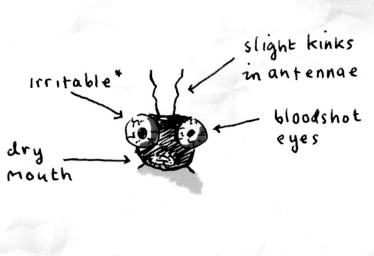

irritable*

slight kinks
in antennae

dry
mouth

bloodshot
eyes

Fig.2 How to tell if
a fly is TIRED

* Always arguing with wife.

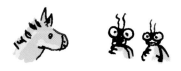

So he offered to babysit Maggot
for them so they could have
a night off.

'How about tonight?' said Fly,
grabbing his coat.

'Um... OK,' said Tim,
taken aback slightly by Fly's
keenness.

'See you later!'
he said ...

but they had already gone.

WAH!
WAH!
WAH!

Straight away, Maggot
woke up and started crying.

[Tim could hear him on the baby listening device.]

So Tim turned the listening
device off.

'That's better,'
thought Tim
the Tiny Horse.

Then he felt a little guilty.

Tim went and got
the screaming Maggot
from his cot...

and walked him up ...

and down.

Pretty soon Maggot was
fast asleep.

Until Tim put him
back in his cot...

at which point
he woke up...

and started
screaming again.

Tim wasn't sure...

but this screaming seemed
louder than the last lot.

Tim walked Maggot up and down
again...

but every time he tried
to put Maggot down he
started screaming.

Tim tried everything to
get Maggot off to sleep.

He tried counting
sheep out loud...

but fell asleep himself...

only to be woken   WAH!
by Maggot's   WAH!
screaming.   WAH!

He tried feeding him...

Gulp!
Gulp!
Gulp!

and even sang
him a lullaby.

[Being an orphan, Tim didn't
know any lullabies and so had
to make one up.]

Go To Sleep Little Maggot

words & music T.T.Tiny-Horse

Go to sleep little maggot
Please don't cry
Stop that racket I beg of you
And one day you'll be a fly.

Chorus
Oh where are your parents?
Surely they can't be much longer!
It's doing my head in
I'm never having children
If it's like this.

Yes, it wasn't great, but it
did the trick.

Until Tim put Maggot back in his cot.

'Scream!'
        bellowed Maggot.

'Sshut up!'
    bellowed Tim
    the Tiny Horse
(completely blowing his top).

Unfortunately...

Fly and his wife had returned home at this point and were in the front room with the baby listening device.

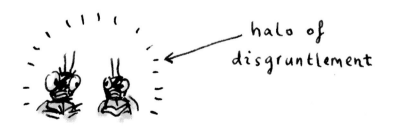

halo of disgruntlement

Tim wasn't employed
as a babysitter again.

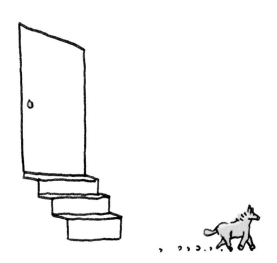

And from then on
Maggot always eyed
him with some suspicion.

'It's probably for the best,'
thought Tim the Tiny Horse.

'After all...'

' know your strengths. '

tim
gets a pet

With Fly now a family man...

Tim found that he had a bit
more time on his hands.

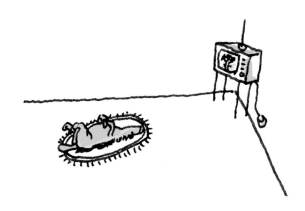

And when there was nothing
on the box he would feel...

bored ...

or worse — lonely.

(but never sorry for himself -
he was just putting that
sad face on for the picture.)

One bank holiday monday, whilst taking a stroll he saw a man walking his dog.

'Humans have pets for company!' he thought.

'That is exactly what I should do!'

... and he headed off

to the pet shop.

Unfortunately all the pets in the shop were rather too big. Some of them were downright frightening.

Especially the dogs.

Even the hamsters were the size of elephants to Tim the Tiny Horse.

PETS 'R' US

'Ho·Hum,' thought Tim the Tiny Horse.

'It looks like I must settle
for a life on my own.'

Just then, he spotted a greenfly
snacking on the stem of a flower.

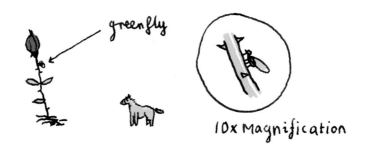

greenfly

10x Magnification

Tim got chatting to the greenfly
(who didn't seem to be that bright).

vacant-looking eyes

'I don't suppose you'd be my pet?'
asked Tim the Tiny Horse.

'sure, why not?' said the
greenfly.

'Great!' said Tim.
'What's your name?'

'George!'
said the greenfly.

And with that, using a piece
of cotton as a lead, Tim
took his new pet home.

tim and george get to know each other better

It turned out that Tim the Tiny Horse and George the Greenfly had quite different tastes.

Tim liked to eat
Hula Hoops and
sugar lumps...

whilst George liked to
drink **SA P**.

Tim liked to play swingball...

whilst George liked to
drink SAP.

Tim had an interest in current affairs...

whilst George liked
to watch 'Emmerdale'...

whilst drinking SAP.

As alluded to earlier, George
didn't seem to have a
particularly high IQ.

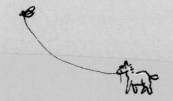

'What's that?' said George,
pointing up at the sky.

'It's the sky,'
answered Tim.

 'Big, isn't it?'
said George.

'Well spotted,' said Tim,
a hint of sarcasm creeping
into his voice.

'what's the sky for?'
asked George the Greenfly.

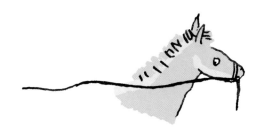

'Um ... it provides us
with a̲i̲r̲,' said Tim,
hopefully.

'What's air?'
    asked George.

'Is that some <u>SAP</u> I can see
over there by that bush?'
said Tim the Tiny Horse.

And George bounded over to
the bush to investigate.

mmm....sap!

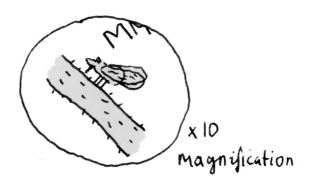

x 10
magnification

On George's first night at
Tim's house, Tim had made
him a bed from four bobbles
off a jumper.

But every time Tim put George
into his bed George would climb
up...

onto the end of Tim's bed.

If Tim returned George
to his bed...

out he would pop.

After five of these episodes...

Tim gave up.

'This pet lark is proving
to be quite a strain,'
he thought.

He looked down at George
asleep on the end of his
bed and had to admit...

he was already quite
fond of him.

'A greenfly is for life...
not just for bank holiday
Monday.'

tim gets
all capitalist
on us

Tim the Tiny Horse had never
had much in the way of
material goods.

So imagine his excitement when he received a cheque for a considerable sum of money from sales of his book.

'I should be careful with this money,' thought Tim the Tiny Horse.

'This sort of luck
doesn't come along
every day...'

'I should invest it...

...in a buy-to-let flat!''

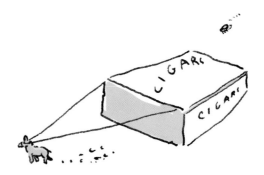

He went straight out and bought himself an empty cigar box...

and set about converting it
into a 'Loft-style' appartment.

He'd learnt from the T.V.
that it was important to
keep things neutral.

So he painted the inside
of the box with
Tipp-Ex.

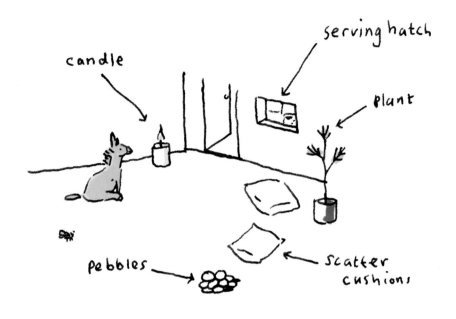

candle

serving hatch

plant

pebbles

scatter cushions

As he surveyed his handiwork
he could almost hear the light,
Jazz-funk music that they
always play over the post-
makeover footage.

'I won't have any problem
shifting this,' he thought.

within a couple
of days a ladybird turned up;
it seemed her own house had
burnt down.

'Is that a greenfly?'
said the ladybird,
looking at George...

and licking her lips.

'Yes, but you wouldn't want to eat him ... he's ill,' lied Tim. 'Listen, take the flat rent-free until you're back on your feet,' he said, taking pity on the ladybird.

So, not only had he spent
a lot of money on the refurb
[Tipp-Ex isn't cheap, you know] ...

he now wasn't getting any
money in to cover his costs.

A couple of weeks later
Tim the Tiny Horse received
a complaint from the
neighbours ...

that the ladybird had had
rather too many guests...

many of whom
had stayed overnight.

When he went to visit
the property...

he found fifteen
juvenile ants living there!

Inside there was utter chaos!

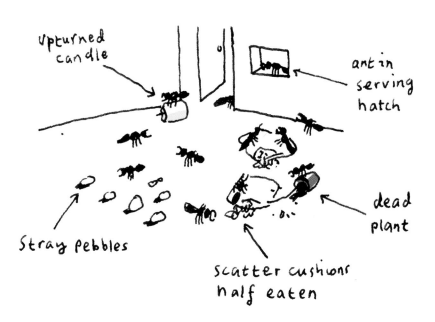

upturned
candle

ant in
serving
hatch

Stray Pebbles

scatter cushions
half eaten

dead
plant

It seemed that the Ladybird
had sub-let it.

'What a nice way

to repay kindness!'

thought Tim the Tiny Horse.

With the help of Fly and a trail of
sugar, Tim managed to get the
ants to leave his cigar-box
apartment.

Tim's experiences in the property
market had been something of
a _let-down_.

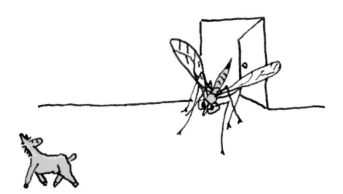

so he flogged the flat to
a daddy long legs.

Sometimes it's just nice to
know your money's safe.

tim loses george

One morning when Tim the Tiny
Horse took George the Greenfly
his usual bowl of sap he
didn't stir.

When the bowl was
still full of sap at lunchtime...

Tim started to get a little
concerned.

George was very still...

and nothing Tim did...

would wake him up.

Tim called the vet, who quickly
worked out that George the
Greenfly had, in fact...

died.

'I'm afraid he's dead,' said
the vet ...

and handed Tim a rather
large bill.

Tim was very upset...

not just at the bill...

but at losing his trusted

(sort of) pet.

Tim tried to cheer himself up
by imagining George in heaven...

fluttering about...

and drinking as much sap
as he wanted.   mmm....sap!

There was a small funeral for
George. All Fly's family came
(even Chenille).

Fly's mum sang 'The circle of Life'... which was one of George's favourites.

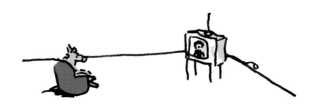

Tim found there were advantages to not being a pet owner again.

For instance, Tim didn't have to worry about taking George out for walks...

or keeping the larder
stocked with fresh supplies
of sap.

But whilst George wasn't
the world's greatest
conversationalist...

and had rather narrow
interests (i.e. sap)...

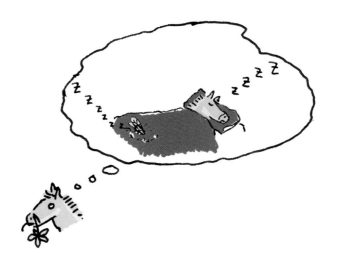

he had a certain <u>presence</u> ...

and Tim missed the little greenfly very much.

So he got another one
and called it...

George the Second!